To Mom and Dad, whose love and encouragement
have rained down in my life like a flood.
C.B.

"Love the Lord your God with all your heart and with all
your soul and with all your strength and with all your
mind,' and, 'Love your neighbor as yourself.'"

LUKE 10:27

ZONDERKIDZ

Get Me to the Ark on Time
Copyright © 2010 by Cuyler Black

Requests for information should be addressed to:
Zonderkidz, Grand Rapids, Michigan 49530

Library of Congress Cataloging-in-Publication Data
Black, Cuyler.
    Get me to the ark on time / written by Cuyler Black.
      p.   cm.
      Summary: A flamingo, continually interrupted by an anteater, tells a story
of two giraffes on Noah's ark who attempt to rescue a pair of turtles in danger
of being trapped outside as the waters rise.
      ISBN 978-0-310-71633-4
      1. Animals—Fiction. 2. Noah's ark—Fiction. 3 Deluge—Fiction. 4. Christian
life—Fiction. 5. Humorous stories.] I. Title.
PZ7.B556Get2010
[E]—dc22
                                       2008048894

All Scripture quotations unless otherwise noted are taken from the *Holy Bible, New
International Version®*. NIV®. Copyright © 1973, 1978, 1984 by International Bible
Society. Used by permission of Zondervan. All rights reserved.

Editor: Mary Hassinger
Art direction and design: Kris Nelson

Printed in China

10 11 12 13 14 15 /GPC/ 10 9 8 7 6 5 4 3 2 1

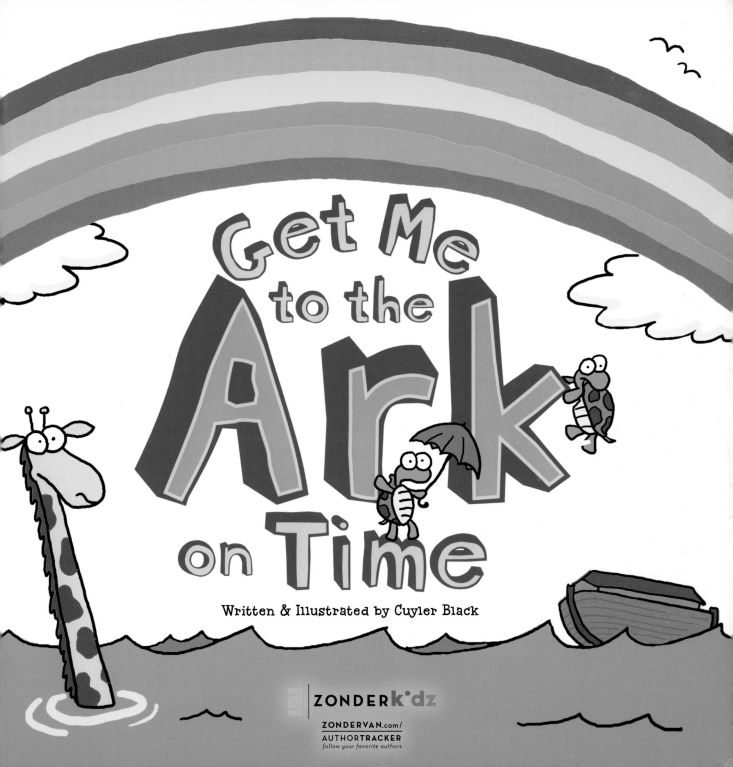

Get Me to the Ark on Time

Written & Illustrated by Cuyler Black

ZONDERk**i**dz

ZONDERVAN.com/
AUTHORTRACKER
follow your favorite authors

God sent two of every kind: elephants... tigers... bats... snakes... kangaroos... eagles... butterflies... crocodiles... polar bears... flamingos... raccoons...

The lion made sure that he and his mate were the first to get on board. He also insisted that they would be the first to get off the boat when it found dry land.

The giraffes had the hardest time on the ark. Their legs and necks were so long that they just couldn't get comfortable.

That does NOT look relaxing.

The other animals laughed at the giraffes' efforts. This hurt the giraffes' feelings more than the ceiling hurt their heads.

– Ow!

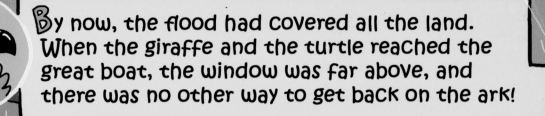

By now, the flood had covered all the land. When the giraffe and the turtle reached the great boat, the window was far above, and there was no other way to get back on the ark!

Oh no! Is that the end? Please tell me that's not the end!

It's not the end! There's more!

With its last strength, the giraffe in the water stretched up its long neck as far as it could. The giraffe on the ark stretched down its long neck as far as it could. The second turtle climbed up to safety.
Just when the giraffe was too tired to swim any longer...

There was a rescue!

At last the giraffes and turtles were all safe on the ark. The other animals cheered for the remarkable giraffes. No one laughed at them anymore.

Nothing pleases God more than when his creatures show love for one another. You giraffes will be rewarded for your great love shown toward the turtles. You will be the first two animals to set foot on the new land God has given us.

Check out Cuyler Black's other funny books and products!

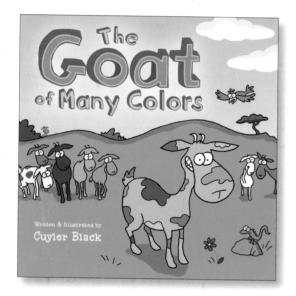

The Goat of Many Colors
978-0-310-71634-4
A creative twist on the story of Joseph and the coat of many colors. Children will learn that God gives each of us special gifts.

Send-A-Laugh Postcards
- Church Life Cartoon Postcards
- Special Occasion Cartoon Postcards
- Old Testament Cartoon Postcards
- New Testament Cartoon Postcards

Each of these 32-page books includes 30 postcards that can be torn out and mailed. Each of the 120 original cartoons stand alone as a lighter, humorous look at faith while keeping a respectful tone.

See more Cuyler Black creations at Inheritthemirth.com

What's that Funny Look on Your Faith?
978-0-310-81397-2
A Far Side-type comic romp through the Bible. Young and old will find it laugh-out-loud funny and a great way to present faith to those who think believers need to "lighten up!"